Know About Tuberculosis

Know About Tuberculosis

Margaret O. Hyde

Walker and Company
New York

The author wishes to thank the many people who contributed to this book. The following were especially helpful: Arthur C. Aufderheide, M.D., School of Medicine, University of Minnesota; Elizabeth H. Forsyth, M.D.; Ruth K. Kasloff, American Lung Association; and Roy Raney, National Jewish Center for Immunology and Respiratory Medicine.

First published in the United States of America in 1994 by Walker Publishing Company, Inc.

Published simultaneously in Canada by Thomas Allen & Son Canada, Limited, Markham, Ontario

Library of Congress Cataloging-in-Publication Data
Hyde, Margaret O. (Margaret Oldroyd)
    Know about tuberculosis / Margaret O. Hyde.
        p.   cm.
    Includes bibliographical references and index.
    ISBN 0-8027-8338-4. — ISBN 0-8027-8339-2 (reinforced)
    1. Tuberculosis—Juvenile literature.   [1. Tuberculosis.
2. Diseases.]   I. Title.
RC311.H93   1994
616.9'95—dc20   94-26288
                                                 CIP
                                                 AC

Illustrations on pages 19 and 31 by Scott D. Wilson.

Chart on page 77 appears courtesy of National Institute of Allergy and Infectious Diseases, National Institute of Health; chart on page 93 appears courtesy of Centers for Disease Control.

Printed in the United States of America
10 9 8 7 6 5 4 3 2 1

Contents

1.

Kids Can Get Tuberculosis

Tiffany is a ten-year-old with AIDS and tuberculosis (TB). Everyone in her class knows how she got AIDS. She had a blood transfusion when she had an operation after an automobile accident. What no one seems to be able to figure out is how Tiffany got tuberculosis.

Tuberculosis? "You can't get that today," says a twelve-year-old girl, who doesn't have the facts straight.

"People had tuberculosis when my great-grandmother was living," says a fifteen-year-old, who is quite right. Then she adds, "No one has it now." But she is wrong about this.

"Remember when the Christmas Seals sent out by the American Lung Association were called TB seals?" asks an elderly woman. "They really helped to get rid of that awful disease." The seals helped raise money to fight TB, but tuberculosis did not disappear.

Tuberculosis is one of the most feared and widespread diseases that has ever threatened humans. It is a disease that is spread from one person to

1907

circa 1920

The first Christmas Seals in America were designed and sold by Emily Bissell for a penny apiece in 1907. The funds raised kept a tuberculosis sanatorium—the only known method of TB treatment at the time—from closing. Today's Christmas Seals, mailed to 40 million homes nationwide, continue the tradition of fighting lung disease. (Reprinted with the permission of the American Lung Association)

4

another through the air, and, less often, through beverages and food. In the United States, from 10 million to 15 million people are infected with the germs that cause it, but only about 10 percent of them will get sick from it. Once a person is infected, however, the risk of developing active TB remains with the person throughout his or her life.

For many years, even doctors believed that the battle against TB was won. But after a thirty-year decline in the number of cases, tuberculosis is increasing, both in the United States and around the world. The year 1993 brought the first reverse in the upward trend in the United States, but some experts think the figures are wrong. World-wide there may be 10 million new cases by the year 2000. In Africa, where there are not enough hospitals to care for the sick and where drugs to fight tuberculosis are scarce, the disease kills about 500,000 people a year. Although there are not as many cases of active tuberculosis in most places as there are in Africa, about one-third of the world's population is infected. In April 1993, the World Health Organization declared the recent rise in the number of tuberculosis cases a global emergency.

Even though tuberculosis is a disease that can be prevented, it now kills about 3.3 million people worldwide each year. The cause of TB is known, and there is a cure for most cases, so something can be done to control the spread of this disease. But without immediate action, it could kill over 30 million people around the world in the next decade. No wonder health experts are calling for more efforts to prevent it through education and tests to identify it so treatment can begin early.

Most people have heard of tuberculosis, but many of them have a vague idea of what it is. Some know it as a disease that affects the lungs, although it can affect other organs, too. Some know that it can be serious enough to cause the death of a person who suffers from it. During the nineteenth century, tuberculosis claimed more lives in the United States than any other disease. Today, it claims more lives around the world than any other infectious disease, one that spreads rapidly from one person to another.

Kevin is a young man who is being exposed to tuberculosis, although he does not know it. He was arrested a few weeks ago after his license was taken from him for speeding. Last week, he drove again while he was drunk and had an accident in which one of the passengers of the other car was killed. Now he waits for his trial, and he may have to wait in the crowded holding pen a long time before his case is heard by the judge. While he waits, he breathes the stale air around him, for there is no window in the cell. He is more worried about getting AIDS than about getting TB, although his chances of getting TB are greater.

Kevin is living in a cramped ten-foot-by-fifteen-foot cage with three other men. Brit, a young man who sits near him, sneezes and coughs often. When he does, he sprays clouds of droplets in the air around him. Many of the droplets are harmless, but some contain the germs—*tubercle bacilli*—that cause TB. Billions of tiny, tiny germs are blown into the air with each cough.

Some of the droplets from Brit's sneezing and coughing reach Kevin's nose, and as he breathes in, they travel into his body along with the air. Many of the droplets are so large, they do not reach the tiny air sacs of his lungs. These drops settle in the trachea, often called the windpipe, which carries air to his lungs. Here his own body kills the germs.

Some of the droplets from Brit's sneezing and coughing fall to the floor. They soon dry out and do no harm. But as some of the droplets fall through the air, they become dry, leaving light, dry material called droplet residue. This floats about in the air for several hours, and Kevin breathes some of it into his lungs.

Certain cells in Kevin's lungs manage to kill germs. But so many germs reach his lungs during the time he spends in the small space that his cells cannot kill them all. The bacilli that survive then multiply in the little balloonlike sacs at the ends of the small tubes that carry oxygen to his lungs. The bacilli kill the cells in which they lie. Kevin's body is now infected, and the germs have taken root.

Tuberculosis bacteria can collect and become walled off in a tiny, hard, grayish capsule known as a *tubercle*. It, and an infection in a nearby lymph node, are the beginning of tuberculosis in Kevin's body.

Although Kevin is infected, he does not have active TB. The germs seem to be waiting until

A doctor at the National Jewish Center for Immunology and Respiratory Medicine uses modern equipment that can quickly identify TB and other mycobacteria. (Courtesy of the National Jewish Center for Immunology and Respiratory Medicine)

they can break out of the tubercle for an all-out assault. If Kevin's body becomes weakened, these bacilli may travel through his blood to other parts of his body. They may attack more areas in his lungs or other organs. But Kevin is healthy. He gives no thought to tuberculosis, for he is only concerned about the trial ahead.

From now on, if Kevin is given a skin test for tuberculosis, the results will show that he is infected. Kevin may not be aware for years that he has been infected with tuberculosis. In fact, he may never know. The germs may never escape from the tubercles. But if he should get sick, and if his immune system is weakened by other diseases, the old germs may become active.

Although about 10 million to 15 million people in the United States have been infected with tuberculosis, only about 10 percent of them ever develop the active form. These are usually people who are poorly fed and are exposed to tuberculosis over a period of time by family members, people with whom they work, or classmates. Those who are old and have weakened immune systems are most likely to develop active tuberculosis, or tuberculosis disease.

Tuberculosis is most apt to take root in people who live in crowded spaces, such as prisons, homeless shelters, and crowded apartments, and those who are in weakened physical conditions. Alcoholics and other drug abusers are candidates for active tuberculosis. Many immigrants from areas such as Latin America, Asia, and Africa, where many people have TB, are infected. When they struggle for existence in the crowded cities of their new land, their disease often becomes active. People with other diseases, such as diabetes, certain types of cancers, and especially AIDS, are at high risk of having active TB.

There has been a striking increase in tuberculosis among the elderly, especially in nursing homes. Some older people are surprised to find that the only medical test they need to enter certain retirement communities is one for tuberculosis.

Have you been tested for tuberculosis? Many doctors are including tests for TB along with the shots they give children to prevent measles, mumps, tetanus, typhoid, and diphtheria. You probably did not get a shot to prevent TB, but you may have had a test on your skin to see whether or not you were ever exposed to the germs. While only a small percentage of the world's children are infected with tuberculosis, health experts are worried because that number is increasing. Today, children under five are getting the disease at the same rate as people between the ages of fourteen and twenty-four.

Campaigns to prevent and cure TB in the past were hailed as triumphs in medicine, but today TB could be a dangerous threat. In many parts of the world, it is becoming known as a disease out of control. Tuberculosis is being called the comeback killer because there are new strains that resist the drugs that once cured it. But most cases of tuberculosis can be prevented.

What can you do to avoid the threat of an old disease that is creating new problems? Knowing about TB is a first step.

2.

The Many Faces of TB

*T*uberculosis is an ancient disease that is caused by a kind of bacterium, *Mycobacterium tuberculosis*, that may have been in the mud of the earth even before human life appeared. It is difficult to imagine men, women, and children who lived in the Stone Age coughing, sneezing, and wasting away from the same disease that was so common in the days of our grandparents' youth, but there is good evidence that they did.

Since tuberculosis can gouge large holes in bones, especially in the bones of the spine, old skeletons tell the tales of its presence. TB also causes ulcers on the ends of the bones of the arms and legs, and these changes can be seen in skeletons, too.

One of the earliest known cases of tuberculosis may have been found in the skeleton of a young man who lived in Heidelberg, Germany, about 7,000 years ago. Some scientists believe that two of the bones in his spine were affected by tuberculosis, but not all scientists agree with this finding. In another case, a young man whose skeleton was found in a cave in Italy died when he was about fifteen years old. Scientists do agree that the bones in his spine show that he had tuberculosis. He lived and died about 6,000 years ago, during the Stone Age. These are just two prehistoric examples of tuberculosis. There are many others.

Tuberculosis was probably a common disease in ancient Egypt. The holes it causes in the spinal bones make the upper back collapse, and make a person bend so that there is a hunch in the back. Egyptian artists drew many pictures of hunchbacks on the walls of tombs. The bones of Egyptian mummies also appear to have been damaged as a result of tuberculosis.

Throughout the centuries, tuberculosis spread through Europe. Ancient bones in Asia and in Africa tell the tale of widespread tuberculosis in those parts of the world, too. The Greeks and Romans of early times wrote about the tragedies it caused in their culture.

Although Columbus and other early European explorers are often blamed for bringing tuberculosis to the New World, there is evidence that Native Americans suffered from it long before Columbus reached them. Since some groups had a custom of piling the skeletons of their dead in huge receptacles, it was easy for scientists to examine their bones and see that large numbers of Native Americans of ancient times had tuberculosis. In 1994,

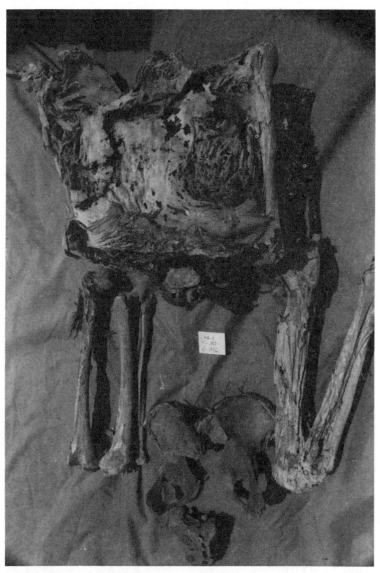

Tuberculosis was identified in the remains of this ancient mummy from Peru. (Courtesy of Arthur C. Aufderheide, M.D.)

scientists in Duluth, Minnesota, reported that they had isolated genetic material from fragments of the tissue of a Peruvian mummy that dates from before the time of Columbus and identified the germ that causes tuberculosis.

Records show that by the middle of the seventeenth century, one in five deaths was due to tuberculosis. Millions in the British Isles and on the continents of Europe and North and South America died from it during the next 200 years.

Epidemics of the Black Death (bubonic plague) and Asiatic cholera during past centuries killed huge numbers of people quickly, but tuberculosis was a slower death. It was often called the White Plague, probably because of the pale skin of Caucasians who wasted away from it. During the end of the nineteenth century, there was a fear that tuberculosis would destroy the civilization of Europe.

Tuberculosis did, and still does, attack many different parts of the human body. Many people think only of pulmonary tuberculosis, the kind that attacks the lungs, as this is the most common form today.

The tuberculosis bacteria grow very slowly in a spot on the lung, in a collection that is somewhat like a cheesy boil. These boils look somewhat like tubers—potatoes, for example, are tubers—so the disease became known as tuberculosis, a term that has replaced the old-fashioned name of consumption. Although the body walls off some of the bacteria, when active germs escape through the coating that surrounds them, the disease spreads. It may spread slowly through the lungs, scarring them and causing the body to waste away as it does. When the bacteria attack blood vessels in the lungs, patients cough up blood, often leaving a bright red spot on the pillow. This is a well-known sign of tuberculosis. When a patient is near death, there is a high, consuming fever, the

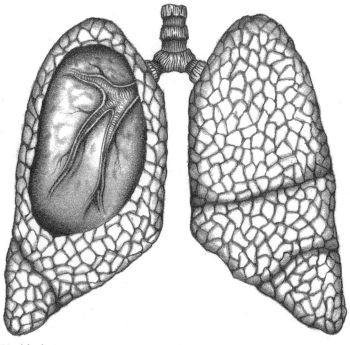

Healthy lungs

symptom that gave this kind of tuberculosis the name consumption. The germs could, and often did, spread from the lungs via the blood to other organs of the body. No organs are immune.

The marks left by tuberculosis were recognized recently in ancient skeletons because of the way TB attacked the bones. Many people suffered through the years from this form of tuberculosis, in which pus would find its way from the cavities in the bones to the skin.

Scrofula, which is tuberculosis of the lymph glands of the neck, was a common name for the disease in the sixteenth, seventeenth, and eighteenth centuries, when no one knew it was related to consumption. It was sometimes called the king's evil, because of a ceremony in which kings touched the people who suffered from scrofula. In those days, kings were believed to have healing powers received from God. Sometimes the swollen glands in the necks of people with scrofula did become smaller after the king's touch. These cures may have occurred because people traveled long distances in the fresh air to reach the monarchs, or because of the faith they had in the king's healing powers. In any case, the practice continued until the end of the eighteenth century.

Inflammation of the coverings of the brain and spinal cord, known as *tuberculosis meningitis,* was a severe form of tuberculosis. It frequently followed *miliary tuberculosis*, in which small nodules of the bacteria were scattered through the bloodstream.

Tuberculosis that affected the skin of the face caused a horrible condition called *lupus*. In the early stages, red marks and thickening of the nose and cheeks made the person appear wolflike. In the disease's severe form, a patient's nose, eyes, cheeks, and ears were partly destroyed, so that he or she looked like a living skull. Some people who suffered from this form of tuberculosis were so ugly that they lived indoors, hidden from the outside world.

Before a cure was found, the young spines of many children collapsed from TB, making hunchbacks common. Tuberculosis of the spine is also known as *Pott's disease* and *gibbus*. Millions of children were crippled by TB of the hip joints, shoulders, and arm and leg bones. Serious cases of diarrhea can result from tuberculosis in the intestines.

In some patients, tuberculosis destroyed the voice box, so that sufferers could only whisper, and even this was painful. Renal tuberculosis affects the kidneys. These are just some of the organs that were commonly infected before a cure was found.

Not only the place but also the rate at which tuberculosis attacked the human body varied. Sometimes tuberculosis acted quickly. When it destroyed the lungs in a few months, it was known as galloping consumption, although there is some question about whether or not some people had been suffering from the disease for a long time before being diagnosed. At the other extreme were cases in which patients managed to complete a normal life span. But tuberculosis usually meant a slow death, and it struck hardest among the young.

A number of other microorganisms (microbes) closely related to the kind that causes tuberculosis in humans are still found in nature. The one that causes tuberculosis in humans, *Mycobacterium tuberculosis,* has more than thirty relatives that are part of the *Mycobacterium tuberculosis* complex. Their names all begin with *"Mycobacterium."* These diseases related to tuberculosis are known to infect a variety of animals, and they have done so from ancient times to the present.

Cows can get a disease known as bovine tuberculosis (caused by *Mycobacterium bovis*), which was much more common long ago. If a cow's udder was infected, the germs got into the milk when the farmer milked her. Humans got tuberculosis from drinking milk, as well as from eating meat. For a period of time, investigators thought that humans could not contract the disease from cows, but it was learned that tubercular cows produced milk that made children tubercular.

Beginning in 1917, cows whose skin tests showed that they had bovine tuberculosis were killed. This eliminated the disease from herds, and the process of pasteurization, in which milk is heated to a temperature that kills the germs in it, assures that people who drink milk today will not be infected. Cows are still checked to make certain they are free of tuberculosis and other diseases, but people who drink raw milk cannot be certain that it is germ-free. We seldom think of the possibility of getting tuberculosis from milk today, but you may wish to ask your grandparents if they remember the words "tuberculin tested" on the labels of their milk bottles.

There is some concern today about a potential threat of bovine tuberculosis from cattle imported from Mexico. Although most people cook their meat well enough to kill the tuberculosis bacteria, those who do not could become infected by eating infected meat. People who work in places where cattle are fed and where meat from cattle with tuberculosis is packed may be at risk, too.

Game ranchers, who raise elk and related animals in restricted areas, are experiencing a widespread outbreak of bovine tuberculosis across America. Wildlife conservation experts are concerned that tuberculosis might spread from elk in the crowded game ranches to elk that live in the wild.

One form, commonly called the vole bacillus, has been found in rats, mice, and their relatives.

Mycobacterium avian complex, also called avian bacillus, is the germ that infects some birds and poultry. It is also the TB bacterium that is most common in people with AIDS. Doctors are using a drug to try to prevent avian tuberculosis from developing in people who carry the AIDS virus. And although it is a rare, noncontagious strain, in recent years some young people who are not infected with HIV have also contracted avian TB.

Mycobacterium tuberculosis can, and probably did, attack every organ of the human body. Before scientists learned about the cause of tuberculosis, many of its forms were not recognized. No one knew that a person who breathed the bacteria might years later develop one of the many kinds of tuberculosis that plagued men, women, and children through the ages.

3.

Can You Get TB by Riding the Bus?

Suppose you have been riding on the school bus with Chad. He is in the hospital now, and you hear that he has broken his leg. While he was at the hospital, a doctor ordered tests to see if Chad's cough was caused by tuberculosis. The report that came back showed that it was. The man who shared the hospital room with Chad was moved to another room so that he would not be exposed to more of Chad's germs.

How much were you exposed? You saw him on the bus each morning and each afternoon for months, and sometimes he sat next to you. You remember that he coughed a lot, but you thought he had a bad cold that would not go away. You were afraid that he was spreading his cold germs to you, but you did not get a cold. Was he spreading the germs that cause tuberculosis?

The answer to that question is yes, but it does not mean that you are infected. It is true that billions of bacteria that cause tuberculosis get into the air when a person coughs, sneezes, sings, or even talks. They are smaller than you can imagine.

Some of the bacteria do dry out and float about in the air, where they may survive for a long period of time. But most people who breathe in these germs do not become infected because cells in their bodies protect them.

Some people think that TB can be spread through touching clothing and other things that have been touched by a person who has active TB. People wrongly thought that about AIDS, too. Today, we know that tuberculosis is not spread through touching things that belong to a person who has it.

Many years ago, ideas about tuberculosis differed greatly. Long ago, in some parts of the world, the fear of getting TB from another person was great. Barbers refused to cut the hair of people who were known to have TB. It was believed that tuberculosis germs could stay in sick people's houses even after the people died. Sometimes sick men, women, and children were turned out of their rooms and apartments, along with all of their belongings. One man was ordered to burn his carriages because a woman with TB had been riding in them. Even the walls of a sick person's room were thought to spread this dreaded disease, and the wallpaper was stripped from them.

In other places, and in other times, the spread of tuberculosis was blamed on different things.

Many doctors blamed tuberculosis on a defect inherited from parents and grandparents.

In the case of Ralph Waldo Emerson, a nineteenth-century American famous for his poems and essays, consumption, as TB was then called, was traced through many generations of the family. Stories were told of people who suffered from the disease after caring for their relatives. Instead of thinking that they were infected directly by these relatives, the idea that the disease ran in families persisted.

Today we know that bacteria cause tuberculosis. But even though one does not inherit tuberculosis, heredity may play some part in the way a person's body copes with being exposed to the disease. The amount of time that a person is exposed to the germs plays a part, too.

Suppose you are an attendant on an airline crew with Cindy, who has active tuberculosis, but she does not know it. (Many people with active tuberculosis do not appear sick in the early stages.) You are on many transatlantic flights with Cindy. About half the air you breathe in an airplane is recycled, so the bacteria that cause tuberculosis come back into the cabin again and again. Might you inhale enough to become infected?

You hear that Cindy is sick; there is a rumor that she has tuberculosis. When you visit your doctor, he tests you to see if you have been infected.

Your test for tuberculosis is positive, and you feel frightened. But your doctor assures you that you will probably never develop the disease. Even though you are infected, the disease is not in an active stage because your immune system keeps it under control. You are not sick and you cannot spread the tuberculosis microorganisms.

What about your friends who have been working with Cindy, too? They are all being tested, and no one is suffering from active tuberculosis. The passengers on the plane, and flight attendants who spend little time with Cindy, are hardly at risk. A healthy adult who spends twenty-four hours a day for two months with a contagious carrier has only a 50 percent chance of becoming infected. It is rare (though not impossible) for a person to get tuberculosis from a single contact.

In Cindy's case, the bacteria that cause tuberculosis became active because her immune system could not fight them the way it should have. Cindy was infected with HIV (human immunodeficiency virus), the virus that causes AIDS. Even though she knew that she had HIV and that she would someday suffer from AIDS, it didn't occur to her to worry about tuberculosis.

Cindy knew that she could not spread AIDS though casual contact with the other members of the flight crew or the passengers. She did know that she had tested positive for exposure to tuberculosis many years ago, but there is so little active TB these days, she never considered that she might get sick from it.

Many cases of tuberculosis are related to AIDS. The germs that cause TB find a good home in patients whose immune systems have been weakened by HIV. With the spread of AIDS to millions of people around the world, the infection rate of tuberculosis also began to rise. By 1993, an estimated 4.4 million people worldwide were infected with both TB and HIV.

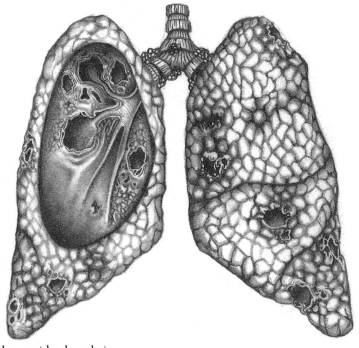

Lungs with tuberculosis

In Africa alone, about 3 million people with HIV are already infected with tuberculosis. Each year about a million new cases of tuberculosis are found in Africa, where HIV is highly prevalent, hospitals are few, and antitubercular drugs are scarce.

Dr. Arata Kochi of the World Health Organization believes that at least half of the AIDS patients carrying the TB bacterium will eventually have active TB. According to Dr. Michael Iseman of the National Jewish Center for Immunology and Respiratory Medicine in Denver, Colorado, almost all people with AIDS who have been infected with TB will develop the active form of the disease.

Most people can avoid getting AIDS by avoiding risky behaviors, such as unprotected sex and using needles to inject drugs. Avoiding the risky behavior that exposes you to tuberculosis is impossible, since that behavior is breathing. Of course, you can usually avoid breathing near someone with active TB if you know that he or she has it. And if you are healthy, you would probably need to breathe near someone who has active tuberculosis for several weeks, or even months, in order to be infected.

Poverty and homelessness are playing a part in the return of active tuberculosis around the world. Shelters for the homeless have been called homes for the bacteria that cause tuberculosis. The rate of infection in homeless shelters in New York City is thought to range from 10 to 43 percent.

Imagine a vast room with 700 cots packed into it. They are in rows, one cot next to the other. In the darkness of night, one hears a variety of noises. Most of the people are sleeping, but some cry out in pain, and others scream as they see a neighbor searching for money and drugs in the clothes they hung at the foot of the beds. Many snore loudly, and the noise of snoring is interrupted by coughing.

In shelters everywhere, people cough and sneeze both day and night, for many of them are infected with tuberculosis that has become active. They spread TB to others in the shelter, many of whom have immune systems weakened from other diseases and from years of poor diet. Alcohol and crack use has played a big part in the lives of some, and this drug abuse has made them more vulnerable to disease.

Jessica is a social worker who tries to help the mentally ill at a large shelter. Many men and women cough and sneeze near her face, and she wonders how many of them have active tuberculosis and are spreading it to her. Recently, TB tests have been required every six months for all social workers in her community. Jessica's most recent test showed that she had indeed been exposed to

TB. This does not mean that she will become sick, but it does show that she might someday.

Today, Jessica is talking to Bo, a man she suspects of having active tuberculosis. Bo does not care much about TB; he is more worried about whether or not he can stay at the shelter. He worries about where he will get his next meal, and whether or not someone will steal his watch and the few dollars he has hidden in his coat lining.

Jessica fills her report with information about Bo's friends, his habits, and any information he is willing to supply. She wants to be able to keep track of him if he does have tuberculosis that needs long-term treatment with a program of taking medicine.

Then Jessica arranges a time for Bo to go to the TB clinic for a test and, possibly, for treatment. The TB clinic is located near the soup kitchen, so that the people who visit the kitchen can be contacted more easily. But many people without places to live move from one shelter or outdoor home to another, and it is difficult to make certain that they are following the treatment program that they need.

Many homeless people have both AIDS and TB. People may be infected with either of these diseases for many years without knowing it, and they can spread them even though they have no symptoms.

Previously, doctors believed about 90 percent of

new cases of tuberculosis developed in people who were exposed much earlier in their lives. Only about 10 percent were thought to develop it from new exposure. But a study published in the *New England Journal of Medicine* in June 1994 found that more than 30 percent of TB cases in New York and San Francisco had been contracted in recent years. Although this new information suggests that TB may be an even greater threat to the general population than was previously believed, it is still unlikely that you could contract TB from riding on a bus.

4.

Fighting the White Plague

*L*ong before tuberculosis had a name, its symptoms were familiar. From ancient times until many years after 1882, when the bacterium that causes it was discovered, patients were subjected to some very strange treatments in efforts to save their lives from the killer disease.

In Greece, in the second century A.D., one "cure" for tuberculosis was rubbing a combination of special oils on the feet of the sick person, wiping them off, and smearing the feet with butter. This may seem silly today, but that was a long time before anyone knew about germs.

Another "cure" was drinking wine made from raisins mixed with the ashes that came from burning the dung of pigs. In ancient Rome, a person who drank a broth in which there was the flesh of a female donkey was supposed to recover from tuberculosis.

Imagine the pain that came from the treatment in which sulfuric acid, a very strong acid that destroys human flesh, was rubbed on the patient's chest in an effort to cure the "wasting disease."

Letting blood flow from the arm of a person suffering from the symptoms we now know as TB was a common practice in fighting the White Plague.

In the early days of medicine, it was common to try to get rid of an illness with poison. Some medicines for tuberculosis contained strychnine, chloroform, cyanide, mercury, alcohol, and morphine. Other medicines, such as brown sugar, were harmless.

In cultures where evil spirits were thought to cause tuberculosis, medicine men tried to chase the spirits away with a variety of plant and animal combinations. Some people wore balls made from the spongy tissue in the stems of certain plants; the balls were dipped in the blood of criminals.

Today, the custom of providing mother's milk for tubercular patients seems strange. However, as late as the nineteenth century, many people accepted the practice of sucking milk from the breasts of women who had just given birth.

People wound skins from cats around their bodies, ate plants grown in special gardens, tied fish around their necks, and did all sorts of strange things in their efforts to prevent death from this mysterious disease. But these methods had little power to cure beyond the help the body gets from the idea that it is being cured.

Years of efforts by doctors and scientists resulted in little progress against the White Plague. About one person in seven was dying from the disease when Robert Koch, a young German doctor, announced in 1882 that tuberculosis was caused by a bacterium.

In a series of experiments in which he crushed the gray tubercles TB germs form, Koch found the tiny rod-shaped bacteria. He called them *tubercle bacilli*, and grew them in the laboratory, something that took considerable work and patience. Most bacteria multiply enough to produce colonies that can be seen after one or two days. Koch watched his experiments day after day; only after ten days could small colonies finally be seen. While much of his work was based on that of scientists who came before him, Koch showed unusual patience and effort.

Koch studied tissue from dead animals and used it to perform experiments on hundreds of laboratory animals. He showed that the disease could be produced by infecting animals with tubercle bacilli taken from another animal. He performed a thorough piece of medical detective work.

On March 24, 1882, Koch's announcement startled the world. When he presented a paper describing his work to the Berlin Physiological Society, the audience was so stunned that they did not even applaud. The bacterium that caused tuberculosis was the greatest killer in the world, but until Koch's work was announced, no one knew that it

Dr. Robert Koch (Reprinted with the permission of the American Lung Association)

existed. At last, the true cause of the disease called the Captain of All the Men of Death was known. Now the search for a true cure could move forward. But the fight against the White Plague was not over, as a cure was still far in the future.

Eight years after Koch discovered the cause of tuberculosis, he believed he had found a substance (a glycerin extract of tubercle bacilli later called tuberculin) that could protect against the disease. This discovery turned out to be useless in curing patients; some even died from it. It did help in the development of a test for active tuberculosis, but real progress was not made until much later.

As long as sixty years after Koch's discovery, there was still no effective treatment. And for many years, the idea that the disease could be spread from one person to another was still not fully accepted. Fourteen years after Koch announced that tuberculosis was caused by a bacterium, Dr. James Tyson, a professor of clinical medicine at the University of Pennsylvania, was not convinced. In his 1896 medical textbook, he wrote: "It is with extreme rarity that a case of tuberculosis in a human being can be traced to another." Many doctors found it difficult to accept the theory that a germ caused tuberculosis. And they continued to try almost anything that they thought might save their dying patients.

Doctors knew that even though there might be

much tissue damage in lungs where many tubercles had formed, the disease destroyed only a small part of the lung tissue. In the early stages of TB, patients could still breathe easily, since humans have far more lung tissue than is actually needed to breathe. But each time germs from tubercles spread to other parts of the lung, and in some cases into the blood, more damage is done.

A number of types of surgery were tried so that the infected areas would be "rested" and patients would not use all of their lungs when they breathed. In one such method, surgeons injected air into the area between the lungs and the wall of the chest to force a lung to collapse. Although a drastic measure, the hope was that the tuberculosis would not spread further if the lung were not used. In another treatment, doctors crushed nerves in a certain area near the lung, paralyzing the muscle on the right or left side of the neck. This resulted in permanent collapse. Other procedures left hope that the lung could be made to function again. In some cases, doctors injected bulky solids into the chest cavity. In another, in an attempt to close the cavities in the lungs, parts of the ribs were removed. This made the patients' chests sink and, of course, made breathing more difficult. But these patients considered themselves to be the lucky ones, for they were still alive. In some cases, the surgery may have resulted in longer lives; in others it might have caused an earlier death. No one knew for certain. But all of these efforts were made in attempts to save people who were dying from TB.

The boldest kind of surgery attempted as an effort to cure tuberculosis was cutting out the infected tissue of the lung. The procedure of trying to get rid of tuberculosis by cutting it out was applied to other organs of the human body, too. Tubercular joints of the arms and legs, kidneys, and other diseased parts of the body were removed in attempts to save lives.

While some people were helped by surgery, millions continued to die from tuberculosis long after Koch had discovered the cause of the disease. Most physicians still considered rest the best medicine. Not only did people try to rest the lungs by surgical means but also there was a great movement toward resting the whole body. The result of this movement was the sanatorium.

5.

TB in the Sanatorium Days

Can you believe that the symptoms of tuberculosis were once considered romantic? In the late eighteenth and early nineteenth centuries, many poets, writers, and musicians suffered and died from active tuberculosis. People who wanted to be considered among the talented and artistic often imitated a tubercular appearance. The paleness, weakness, and weight loss were admired, since tuberculosis was thought to attack only those with a sensitive and creative nature. Some healthy and athletic women used white powder on their faces and acted tired, just to be in fashion.

Later, when tuberculosis was known to be widespread among the poor, pale faces and sunken eyes were no longer considered beautiful. Those with tuberculosis were considered weak and shiftless, although not everyone felt this way. Many religious individuals and groups worked to help the poor who were suffering from tuberculosis.

At the time of the Industrial Revolution in the late eighteenth and early nineteenth centuries, there were great outbreaks of tuberculosis. Huge numbers of people moved from their farms to the city to work in new industries. The workers were close together for long hours in factories, mills, mines, and offices. The germs that caused tuberculosis spread easily from one person to another. Still, most people, even doctors, were totally unaware of the idea of contagion.

Crowded living conditions, poor food, and exhausting physical labor made fertile ground for the spread of tuberculosis, as did child labor, which was common at that time. Young boys and girls worked in mills where stale air smelled of oil from machinery. In some mills, one set of children worked long hours during the day and went to bed at the mills at the end of their day. Other children, who slept during the day, rose from their beds to work all night. The day workers climbed into the same beds that the night workers had left, only to get up and return to work in the morning. It was a common expression in some regions of England that the beds never got cold. There was little thought about the health of the children, or about the coughing that spread tuberculosis from one child to another.

René Dubos, scientist and author of *The White Plague*, tells of a young woman with active tuberculosis who spent her days in bed. She dressed at night and went to parties, where she spread tuberculosis to many others. Another young woman, who coughed almost all the time and sometimes brought up blood from her diseased lungs, enjoyed visiting friends. They sat closer together in small rooms, where stoves kept them warm during the cold days of New England winters. Here she spread the germs to many others, who in turn spread them to their friends. This was typical of the way TB was spread socially. Even in the beginning of the twentieth century, many people were unaware that TB was contagious, and they spread their germs to family and friends.

Many victims of TB received only the care and love of their own families. That may have been the best medicine available, along with fresh air and sunshine. Some rich people, who could afford to build additions to their homes, added an extra floor to the tops of their houses so their loved ones could live in the fresh air and sunshine.

For a long time, life in a sanatorium—a place where patients spent much of their time resting and sleeping in the fresh air—was considered the best way to cure tuberculosis. The first large American sanatorium for tuberculosis patients was built in 1884 by Dr. Edward Trudeau. It was built at Saranac Lake in the Adirondack Mountains of New York, where Dr. Trudeau had himself experienced a return to health.

Saranac became one of the most famous sanatoriums in the United States. It was a place where

Dr. Edward Livingston Trudeau in his laboratory (Reprinted with the permission of the American Lung Association)

the rich, the famous, and the gifted arrived for treatment at the same train station where the coffins of those who had died from tuberculosis were piled for their journey to their families' cemeteries.

Within the next fifty years, the United States had 600 sanatoriums for patients with tuberculosis. In the early years of the twentieth century, most of the sanatoriums were private, but in later years, the great majority were under the control of cities, counties, and states. Private sanatoriums were expensive, while the public ones were more like hospitals.

The sanatoriums served two purposes. In addition to providing what was thought to be the best chance of recovery, they kept the sick patients from spreading their disease to others. This second benefit was not always known.

When the disease was found in a number of members of the same family, physicians suggested that they had an inherited tendency for the disease, or they lived in a bad climate, or they all lived on damp soil, or some other reason. Only a small percentage of doctors believed that tuberculosis was contagious, perhaps because it usually takes more than casual contact for a person to be infected.

Ellie was fifteen years old in 1895. She had spent the last three years taking care of her sick mother,

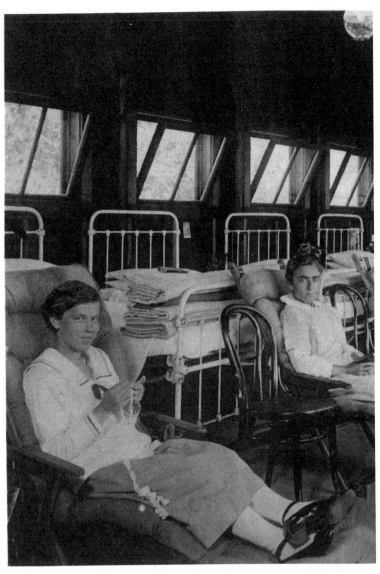

TB patients were treated with rest, fresh air, and occupational therapy in a sanatorium circa 1920. (Reprinted with the permission of the American Lung Association)

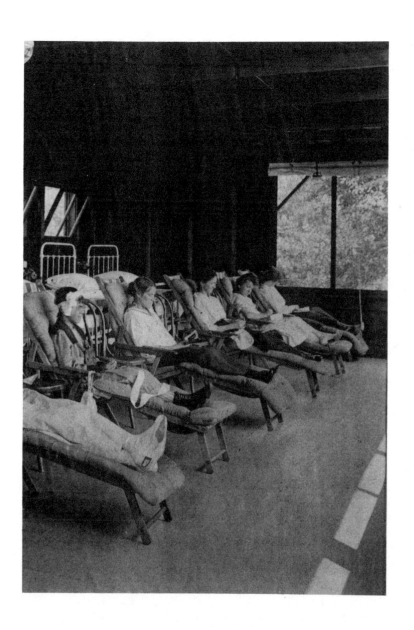

who died from tuberculosis. Now, although she was sad about her mother's death, she was free to begin a life of her own.

Ellie planned to study art, but she did not feel well enough to do much painting. Perhaps she was tired from the burden of caring for her mother—or did she, too, have the dreaded disease that meant an early death? It did not occur to Ellie or to her father that she might have been infected by her mother, even though she did have many of the same symptoms.

On the morning of her fifteenth birthday, Ellie was too tired and too worried to celebrate; she had just noticed a bright red spot of blood on her pillow. This was a well-known symptom of consumption, as tuberculosis was commonly called in those days. Ellie had been coughing and sneezing for months, but during those months she had told herself that she did not have the disease that had killed so many of her young friends. After she saw the blood on her pillow from her nightly spell of coughing, she knew she must tell her father and her doctor about it.

By this time, Ellie already looked like many tuberculosis patients. She was very pale and thin. Her forehead was often covered with drops of sweat, and her cheeks were bright crimson against her white face. Her bright eyes had sunk into her head, and the palms of her hands were dry and hot. She coughed so much that there were times when she could barely talk.

Ellie's doctor realized almost at once that she suffered from TB. He suggested that she be sent to a sanatorium. Although sanatoriums were common in those days, Ellie was sad and frightened about going away. She had to leave her family and friends to live in a place far from home. And she might die in the sanatorium; many people did.

Ellie did not enjoy her life at the sanatorium. She was kept in bed twenty-four hours a day, every day for a full year. She was bathed in bed and was spoon-fed by nurses, and when she needed to urinate or defecate, a cold bedpan was brought to her. The doctors told her that complete rest would help her lungs heal, just as a splint on a broken leg rested it and helped the bone to heal. Ellie found it difficult to believe that talking would hurt, but even that was against the rules, except for short periods of time. She could not read, knit, or do anything other than just lie quietly in bed. She was scolded if she disobeyed these rules, and told that she might lose her bed to someone on the sanatorium's waiting list.

Some patients at sanatoriums did improve with rest and fresh air. But Ellie, like many others whose disease was far advanced, died in spite of the strict and expensive care. Some severely ill patients were released with instructions to seek a

In the 1920s, children at sanatoriums were kept outside whenever possible. (Reprinted with the permission of the American Lung Association)

warmer climate. Actually, these people were sent away, or to their homes, to die.

Tuberculosis sanatoriums were built in a variety of places in many countries. According to some doctors, sea air was best. Others believed in sending patients to a dry climate. Warm places were popular; so were cold. No one really knew what was best, and treatment varied from complete bed rest to programs that included exercise. Pure air, pure water, and pure food were common requirements for patients at a sanatorium.

Many sanatoriums had large porches where patients were kept outdoors most of the time, even when there was snow all around them. At some, patients lived in tents all year—even in winters when the temperature was well below freezing. Staying outdoors, no matter what the conditions, was recommended by many medical experts. Fresh air was thought to help with the supply of oxygen to the lungs. Thus a major part of the treatment in all climates consisted of wrapping patients in blankets and having them rest in reclining chairs in the open air.

Sanatoriums varied greatly in the amount of comfort and attention patients received. Religious organizations and a variety of charities helped some patients who could not afford a private sanatorium and could no longer manage to live at home. As a last resort, when they could find no

Children with TB were often taught in open-air classrooms (top) and were encouraged to take advantage of the fresh air and sunshine as the children pictured above are doing at a TB clinic in Denver in 1924. (Reprinted with the permission of the American Lung Association and the National Jewish Center for Immunology and Respiratory Medicine)

other place, many of the poor consumptives ended their lives in poorhouses.

Many of the sick were bored, lonely, and unhappy. They begged to go home to their families, where they felt they were needed, or where they felt they would be allowed more freedom and better food. Many patients felt neglected and unwanted. Some became restless and suspicious of the treatment they were getting. One woman wrote a letter about her husband, saying that he was not getting enough to eat. She believed that the doctors and nurses did not want the patients to live, so they were starving them to death.

Most sanatoriums shut their doors in the years between 1930 and 1950, for by then it was recognized that a real cure for tuberculosis had been discovered. To this day, no one really knows how much the fresh-air routines of the sanatoriums helped their patients. It is known that TB was responsible for 5 million deaths in the first half of the twentieth century.

6.

Searching for a Cure

*T*oday, your doctor can prescribe over 100 different antibiotics for different illnesses. If you have active tuberculosis, he or she will probably choose the two antibiotics most commonly used. If you take your medicine as directed, you can be almost certain of a cure. But finding the first medicine to halt the tragic progress of tuberculosis was far from easy.

Before a cure was known, the number of deaths from tuberculosis was so great that the disease affected almost everyone in one way or another. The sick lay in hospitals everywhere, wasting away from the last stages of a disease for which there was no help. Doctors felt great hopelessness as they watched their feverish patients suffer with bouts of coughing that they could relieve only with painkillers.

From the time of Koch's discovery of the tubercle bacillus, scientists in many different laboratories were working to find new cures for a variety of diseases, including tuberculosis. One hope lay in the study of microbes, especially microscopic organisms that lived in air and soil and had shown that they could kill germs.

Progress toward a cure for tuberculosis was more difficult than in the case of many other diseases, but it moved forward in bits and pieces. There were scientists who believed that a cure for TB would never be found; they thought nothing would be able to penetrate the heavy, waxy coating of the germ that caused it. And the germ's slow rate of growth made experiments difficult. Anyone trying to find a substance that would kill such a germ needed a great deal of patience.

One discovery built on another as many men and women spent long hours in their laboratories. Many of these scientists had lost members of their families to tuberculosis. They remembered the deaths of classmates as far back as elementary school and they saw the tragic deaths of young people around them. This disease had reached far and wide around the world, infecting and killing people of different races, nationalities, ages, religions, and political beliefs. A cure for TB could end all of this.

By 1932, it was known that tuberculosis germs were killed when added to certain types of soil, but lived when placed in sterile soil. So something in the soil must kill them. But every particle of soil contains thousands of different kinds of microbes. Finding the one that would destroy the slow-growing bacteria that was covered with a heavy waxy capsule was a gigantic task.

By 1939, Selman Waksman, a pioneer in the study of microbes in the soil, had coined the noun *antibiotics*. René Dubos had shown progress in isolating soil microbes able to kill bacteria that caused some kinds of disease. But the tubercle bacilli remained indestructible. Experiments that were expected to produce wonder cures ended in disappointment. The battle against tuberculosis continued on many fronts.

The first real cure for tuberculosis came in 1943. Albert Schatz, a brilliant and dedicated student of Selman Waksman at Rutgers University in New Jersey, made an exciting discovery. He found an antibiotic that would later become one of the most important milestones in the history of medicine. Albert Schatz and his co-workers discovered the microbe that was eventually called streptomycin.

Before it could be tried on animals and eventually used as a medicine, streptomycin had to be concentrated for use in experiments. Schatz went back to his basement laboratory, working night and day to do the job. He even slept on the floor in the corner of his laboratory. At night, when the experiments needed tending, the night watchman in the building would wake him up, and he would work until he could take time off for another

Selman A. Waksman, Ph.D. (Reprinted with the permission of the American Lung Association)

period of sleep. Often, he did not leave the building for days at a time.

When Schatz succeeded in concentrating a small amount of streptomycin, it was ready for testing on live animals at the Mayo Clinic in Rochester, Minnesota. Guinea pigs were the first animals to be used in a long series of experiments in the battle against tuberculosis, for they were known always to get sick and die when injected with the tuberculin bacillus.

At the Mayo Clinic, scientists used the tiny amount of streptomycin sent to them from Rutgers on four guinea pigs. Twelve animals were infected with tuberculosis, and four of them were given the precious streptomycin. Would they be cured? Would the streptomycin really work the way it had in the laboratory?

After fifty-five days, when the supply of streptomycin ran out, the guinea pigs were painlessly killed, and with great excitement the scientists learned that all four animals that had received streptomycin had been cured of tuberculosis.

Many animal experiments followed. Larger amounts of the drug were produced by a company in the business of making medicines. Now tests on humans began. Even though supplies of the drug were still limited, the results were promising. Further testing on guinea pigs, and on humans who had no hope of living without streptomycin, finally established it as the first antibiotic in history to cure tuberculosis.

Unfortunately, the part that Albert Schatz played in the discovery of streptomycin was hardly recognized in the excitement that followed it. Waksman, his teacher and co-worker, who had played a part in the discovery and spread the word about the new drug, received much more of the praise from a grateful world.

Streptomycin was used successfully in the treatment of huge numbers of cases. Word of this new drug gradually spread to Europe, where its ability to halt the disease was considered miraculous. In the United States, the number of cases of tuberculosis fell, but streptomycin did not cure everyone. Some patients even suffered serious side effects from it, such as deafness.

In other countries, new drugs that seemed to cure tuberculosis appeared. They, too, helped only some people with certain kinds of the disease. In Germany after World War II, where tuberculosis was widespread, a new drug, Conteben, was used to treat thousands of people. One outstanding case was that of a woman who had tuberculosis of the skin of the face. She had lived in a sanatorium for many years, and had tried a wide variety of remedies for her badly damaged face. Her left eye had been destroyed, and her face was covered with sores caused by the tuberculosis. She had suffered

This year celebrate with Christmas Seals.®

AMERICAN LUNG ASSOCIATION

80th ANNIVERSARY · 1987 ®

It's a matter of life and breath.®

AMERICAN LUNG ASSOCIATION
The Christmas Seal People ®

(Reprinted with the permission of the American Lung Association)

for thirty years, but Conteben stopped the disease within five months. This, and many other cases, seemed like a miracle to both patients and their doctors. But, like streptomycin, Conteben did not cure everyone.

Other antibiotics that halted tuberculosis followed the discovery of streptomycin, and these helped to decrease the number of cases. As time went on, people in the United States had better food, better health habits, and better hospital care than in earlier times. The disease seemed to be almost conquered. Some of the campaigns to prevent the spread of tuberculosis were winding down. The American Lung Association had sold Christmas Seals, which had raised $20,000,000 to fight tuberculosis in 1950. These seals are still sold, but now they raise money to fight all lung diseases. With the introduction of new drugs to fight tuberculosis, and with stricter isolation of hospital patients with active tuberculosis, the case rate fell.

The rate of tuberculosis reached an all-time low in the United States in 1985, but as we know now, the battle was not completely won. With new strains of the germ, the search for cures continues.

7.

The New Tuberculosis

*F*or many people with tuberculosis, things are not what they used to be. The antibiotics that killed the old strains of the germ are not succeeding in the battle against some of the new varieties. Although the old kind of tuberculosis is still common, the battle against new strains creates a special challenge. Why has tuberculosis changed? Why is it coming back? There are no easy answers to these questions, but some of the reasons are known.

Suppose you have active tuberculosis of the old strain and you do not take medicine for it. There is a 40 percent to 60 percent chance that you will die from the disease. But if you do follow your doctor's orders, there is a very good chance that you will be quite healthy again after you finish taking the medicine.

In the past, more than 90 percent of tuberculosis cases could be cured with medicine, providing it was taken as directed. At one point, there was a goal to eliminate TB in the United States by the year 2010.

"Thanks to successful treatment with antibiotics, tuberculosis is disappearing." Such statements were often made in books about medicine less than ten years ago. New books read differently. Old graphs that show the number of cases of tuberculosis in the United States between 1950 and 1985 have straight lines descending from beginning to end. Then the decrease in the number of cases ended. Beginning around 1985, the incidence of TB in the United States rose until 1992. In 1993, a lower figure might have been due to a problem in reporting or to better prevention methods.

Today, a doctor's prescription might tell a patient to take two drugs, isoniazid and rifampin, for the next six months. In some cases, a third drug, pyrazinamide, is ordered for the first two months. This is a long time to take medicine, especially after a person starts to feel better.

Sometimes people have to take drugs every day for years. Carey is a heroin addict who goes to a clinic every day for a dose of a drug called methadone, which relieves her craving for the illegal heroin. She has been very faithful about going to the clinic, for if she misses a day, she feels ill. Her addiction makes it necessary for her body to have certain chemicals in order to feel normal. She would need larger and larger doses of heroin to feel normal, but in the case of methadone, a steady amount will keep her feeling fine. The methadone

Actual Versus Expected Number of TB Cases in the United States, 1981–1992

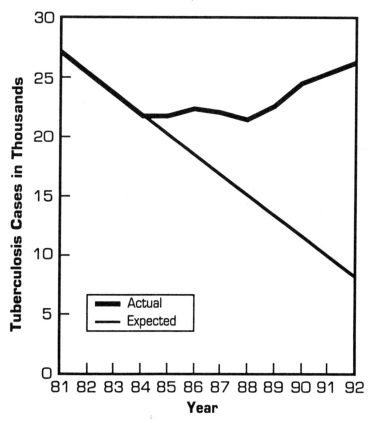

has been prescribed by her doctor to help her while a psychiatrist spends an hour with her every week to help her deal with other problems.

Carey's health has always been one of her many problems. Lately, she has been coughing a great deal, feels tired, is losing weight, and sometimes has a fever. When her doctor tests her for tuberculosis, he finds that the germs in her body have become active. Now she needs medicine for the TB, as well as methadone for her drug problem. She needs to take three more drugs each day.

At the clinic, a nurse watches Carey drink the orange liquid with the methadone in it. No one watches to make sure that Carey takes her medicine for tuberculosis; she must remember this. After the first few months, Carey feels fine. Her symptoms of tuberculosis are gone, and she does not always remember to take the medicine for it. Even though the government pays for her medical bills, Carey forgets everything but her methadone. Carey has almost forgotten about her TB. She is more worried about finding a place to live, getting along with her abusive roommate, keeping up with her job, and finding time to see her doctor about her addiction.

After a few months, Carey begins to have new symptoms of tuberculosis, and this time, they are caused by a different strain of tuberculosis. The drugs that would have cured her first illness, if she had taken them long enough, will not win the battle against these germs. Carey now has a kind of tuberculosis that is called multi-drug resistant (MDR). The doctor will prescribe different antibiotics, all of which can produce serious side effects. This time, Carey will be given these drugs by a nurse at a clinic, which she visits after her trip to the methadone clinic. One of the tuberculosis drugs is injected into her arm by a needle, but she swallows the others. She is in a program called DOT, for "directly observed therapy."

Doctors believe that the strains of TB that are difficult to treat will become common if more action is not taken to prevent their spread. In studies of patients with drug-resistant tuberculosis, only one in ten took their original medicine the way the doctor directed.

Health care workers try a variety of ways to get patients to cooperate. They may visit the patients at home if they miss an appointment. Sometimes, visiting nurses take food baskets, birthday cakes, valentine cookies, flowers from their gardens, or treats for the children. They offer favors in order to get the patients to take their medicine regularly and long enough to do the job of battling TB. In Los Angeles, there is a program for street people in which those who take their pills get vouchers for meals and rooms at a nearby building that has single rooms available. This may seem like an expensive way of treating people, but it costs more than $100,000 to hospitalize a person with multi-drug-resistant TB.

Most people with active TB stop being infectious within days after they start taking medicine. Those patients with drug-resistant tuberculosis, however, can spread the disease for a longer period of time after they start taking medicine. No wonder health care workers are trying various plans to get people to take their medicine for the full amount of time needed to conquer their illness. They want to help the patient get better, and they also want to prevent him or her from developing drug-resistant TB and spreading it to others.

In the spring of 1994, the U.S. Food and Drug Administration approved a pill that combines the power of three antituberculosis medicines. Doctors hope that this will make it easier for patients to complete their treatment and be cured. The consequences of not taking medicine as directed can be severe. Not only is the care of the sick person expensive but also that person may spread the disease to many others. The records of the U.S. Centers for Disease Control (CDC) in Atlanta, Georgia, show an alcoholic man in Mississippi who was being treated for tuberculosis of the lungs. He did not take his medicine regularly, and his wife and son became infected. The illness spread to hundreds of other people, at least twelve of whom had drug-resistant germs. Three of them died. Doctors must report all cases of tuberculosis to the government-run CDC. Recently, many cases show that the new strains of tuberculosis spread more quickly than the kind that can be cured by the more common antibiotics.

Some people think that antibiotics are a magic

medicine that cures everything. They demand that their doctors give them a prescription for an antibiotic every time they have a cold. But antibiotics are effective only against bacteria. Colds are caused by viruses, and taking antibiotics for them—or for other illnesses caused by viruses—will not make you better faster. In fact, it may make it harder to treat other illnesses later. Experts suggest that instead of asking your doctor *for* an antibiotic, you should ask *why* one is being prescribed. The use of unnecessary antibiotics may have played a part in making new strains of TB that are resistant to the antibiotics commonly used for it.

In the United States, the National Institute of Allergy and Infectious Disease is supporting programs to study tuberculosis and develop new tools to recognize it, new vaccines to prevent it, and new ways to educate the public about it. Since one-third of the world's population is infected with tuberculosis, and since new strains of TB are spreading, it is important to know how TB is spread and how to prevent it.

8.

Keeping TB Under Control

A woman in Montana with active tuberculosis did volunteer work at her church and helped with many community activities. She began an epidemic among those with whom she worked.

Of course, the woman in Montana did not know that she had active tuberculosis. She was trying to help people, but she caused many tragedies because she did not recognize the symptoms of tuberculosis. She had been coughing for several months before she asked her doctor why she was coughing so much and feeling so tired. One of the tests he performed showed the reason for her symptoms.

In order to find out if the woman had tuberculosis, the doctor injected a substance under the skin on her arm. He told her to come back to see him in two days so he could examine the results of the test. When the doctor saw the size of the red area on the woman's arm, he ordered further tests. When he was certain that she had tuberculosis, he began treatment with antibiotics. Soon, this woman could no longer spread the disease. After six months or perhaps nine months, her battle with the germs would be over, probably forever.

Prevention of tuberculosis begins with finding out which people have been infected and which have active cases. There were more TB screening programs in the past than there are today. Your parents may remember when all American school-children were given a skin test for TB, known as a *tine test.* A four-pronged device was used to puncture a small area on one arm. After two or three days, the school nurse would examine each child's arm to see if any infection was present. If there was no swelling or redness, or only a small amount, at the places that had been pricked, the person had not been exposed to tuberculosis. If there was swelling and redness in a larger area (about half an inch) within forty-eight to seventy-two hours of the test, the child had been exposed. This did not mean that he or she had TB, but rather that there was a 10 percent chance that the child would develop it someday.

Another tuberculin skin test, the *Mantoux test,* is commonly used today to identify people who have been exposed to the tubercle bacillus. This test, sometimes called the *PPD test,* involves a single needle prick on the arm. The area is examined two or three days later. If a red welt about the size of a pencil eraser forms, the person has been infected at some time in his or her life. But if a

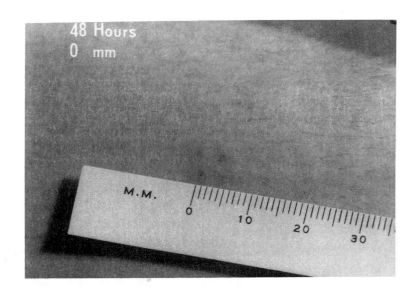

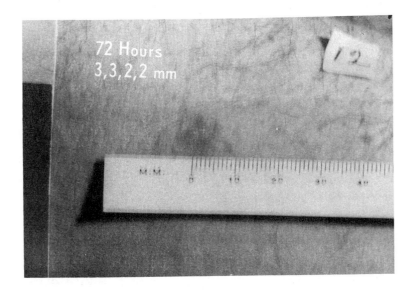

Tuberculosis tine tests after 48 hours and 72 hours. (Reprinted with the permission of the American Lung Association)

person is HIV-positive, the skin test will not always show the presence of the TB germs. Better and faster tests are needed to help in the quick diagnosis of TB.

Doctors cannot learn much about tuberculosis with only a skin test. Further tests, such as chest X rays and laboratory examination of people's germs, are needed to accurately diagnose any kind of active tuberculosis. The skin test only tells doctors that further information is needed. Not long ago, people had chest X rays whenever they went to their doctors for general physical examinations. With the decrease in tuberculosis and attempts to reduce exposure to X rays, this practice stopped. Now, many hospitals X ray incoming patients for TB.

In parts of the world where tuberculosis is common, a vaccine made of weakened germs from TB-infected cows is part of a program to prevent the spread of TB. This vaccine, called BCG (for "Bacillus Calmette-Guérin") has not been used much in the United States, partly because there are questions about its value for adults.

If a person has been vaccinated with BCG and is given a skin test at a later date, the test will show TB exposure even though he or she does not have active TB. There is no reliable method of telling the difference between a positive reaction caused by BCG and one caused by a natural infec-

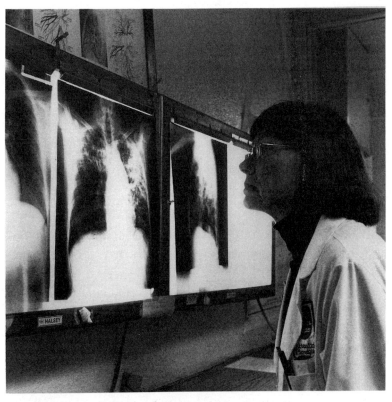

Dr. Anne Davis examines lung X rays for signs of TB. (Reprinted with the permission of the American Lung Association)

tion. This makes it more difficult to screen those who really have active TB, and is another reason that BCG is not widely used in the United States. But the BCG vaccination is now recommended for American infants and children who are at risk of being exposed to anyone with infectious tuberculosis.

In 1994, new studies at Harvard School of Public Health indicated that BCG reduced the risk of active tuberculosis by 50 percent and death by 71 percent. But the widespread use of BCG would make it impossible to detect exposure to tuberculosis by the tuberculin skin test, since everyone who had the BCG vaccine would test positive.

BCG is not recommended for people infected with HIV, so this, too, creates a problem with the wide use of BCG. Many people with HIV are not aware that they carry the AIDS virus. Besides, researchers do not know how long BCG's protection against tuberculosis lasts. There is much to be learned about using BCG in the control of tuberculosis, but scientists are renewing their debate about it. Certainly, new and more effective vaccines are needed to help prevent the spread of this disease.

A new vaccine would be especially helpful to prevent the spread of TB among children who live in crowded conditions. Between 1980 and 1990, cases of tuberculosis among children under four years old in the Bronx section of New York City increased 300 percent. Experts believe this may have happened partly because more people are living in crowded homes. Poor nutrition, poor ventilation, and drug use weaken immune systems and thus play a part in the increase of tuberculosis, too. As these problems continue to get worse, the control of TB becomes more difficult.

Since 1985, when the number of TB cases began to grow, efforts have been made to increase funding for screening, but more money is needed. There are some new programs to make people aware of the way tuberculosis is spread, and to alert them to the new strains that are not cured by the old antibiotics. One new program in the state of New York is an experiment with the use of ultraviolet lights to kill TB germs in shelters in six cities. These lights were used in the past on bed linens in some sanatoriums. Might they help in shelters and other closed areas where many people are crowded together?

The increase in multi-drug-resistant TB is especially high among African-Americans, Hispanics, and other racial minorities in the United States. In 1990, more than 85 percent of the reported cases among children in the United States were among these groups. Skin tests are recommended for all blacks and Hispanics who live in crowded cities, for they are considered to be in danger of infection with tuberculosis. Many of these people have special housing and financial problems that make it difficult for them to follow doctor's orders and for doctors to follow the patients.

Louis came to the United States from Mexico to pick vegetables at farms in California. When he entered the United States, he was supposed to be treated at a local health clinic for his tuberculosis. But Louis moved from farm to farm so much that it was impossible for the people who worked at the health center to follow him. Although he was given medicine and was told to take it every day for six months, Louis felt fine after a few weeks. He forgot about the medicine.

When Louis started to take his pills, some of the germs that caused his symptoms were killed right away. Others, which were stronger, survived. Months later, when these stronger germs had multiplied, Louis started feeling sick again. He visited another health clinic, and he mentioned his TB. The doctor collected some of Louis's sputum—the material that came up from his lungs when he coughed—and had it checked at the medical laboratory. The report showed that Louis had drug-resistant TB. He could not be cured with the same antibiotics that were used to treat the tuberculosis he had when he entered the country.

Some people who are unwilling or unable to take medicine regularly for their multi-drug-resistant

Reported TB Cases Among Children in the United States in 1990

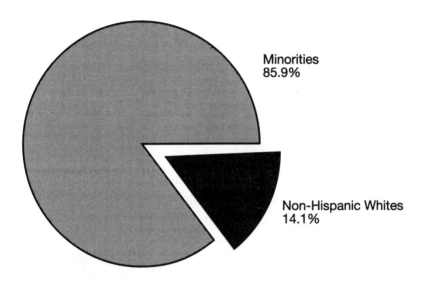

Minorities
85.9%

Non-Hispanic Whites
14.1%

tuberculosis are kept in hospitals, trailers, or other special residences, sometimes against their wishes. They must stay in isolated areas so that they will not spread their disease to others and so that nurses can be certain that they take their medicine the way the doctor orders it.

Keeping patients against their wishes may seem like a mean thing to do, but doctors are not trying to punish these people even though uncooperative patients probably frustrate them. The doctors just want to cure them and prevent them from causing an epidemic of tuberculosis that cannot be cured.

Nurse Helen Infante gives medication to a patient in the TB ward of New York City's Bellevue Hospital. (Reprinted with the permission of the American Lung Association)

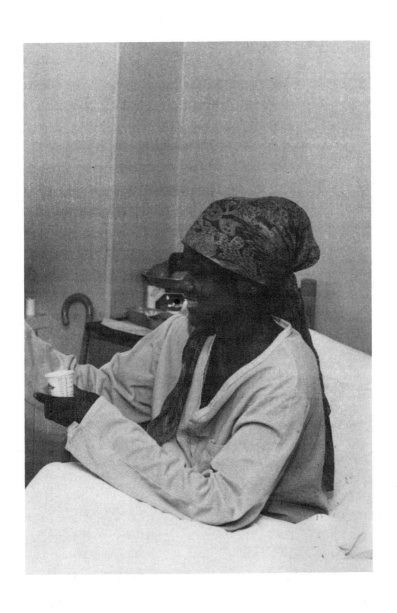

What stops medical workers from quickly finding a vaccine or a cure for the new kind of tuberculosis? The tubercle bacillus is a tricky germ. Dr. George Jacoby, who works at Massachusetts General Hospital, says that "bugs" are always figuring out ways to get around the antibiotics we throw at them. The strong bacteria that survive small doses of antibiotics soon multiply. The descendants of those bacteria are strong as well. Soon there is a new drug-resistant strain. The TB has changed—and comes roaring back.

As mentioned earlier, the bacterium that causes tuberculosis is difficult to study. Most bacteria used in experiments form colonies that can be seen in about eight hours. The tuberculosis bacteria take three to four weeks to grow a similar colony. The waxy coat, which is hard to get past, makes the testing of new drugs difficult. The tuberculosis germs also tend to form clumps, and that makes it hard for scientists to work with them. In addition to these and other problems, protecting laboratory workers from being infected is complicated and expensive. And, at this time, searching for drugs that cure and prevent the spread of other diseases, such as AIDS, is more popular than the study of TB. But now many scientists are sending out warning signs about the risk of TB infection, especially with germs that are not killed by the treatments that worked in the past.

Today, many laboratories around the world are using computer networks to share information about new strains of bacteria and viruses. When medical workers learn about the existence of a new germ early, they have a better chance of learning how to fight it. Volunteers are helping to link laboratories in the United States, South America, Central America, and Asia. But the budget for this work is small, and much more work needs to be done to stop the spread of new diseases.

Although this is not a time to panic about tuberculosis, it is a time to become more serious in efforts to prevent its spread. The World Health

A lab technician prepares cultures for growing the bacteria that cause TB. (Courtesy of the National Jewish Center for Immunology and Respiratory Medicine)

Organization reports that about a third of the world's population is already infected and 8 million people get sick from it each year.

In some countries, $13 will buy the medicine to cure a patient with tuberculosis, but poor countries may not have the money to treat many people. Drug-resistant strains are rising rapidly, so it is no wonder that the World Health Organization is asking for money to finance programs that fight the disease and stop the new strains that might cause a public-health disaster.

In the United States, it costs about $1,000 to treat a person using directly observed therapy. This seems expensive until one compares it with the cost of hospital care for a patient with multi-drug-resistant TB, estimated at nearly $100,000.

What is going to happen if we don't stop the spread of multi-drug-resistant TB? You probably won't catch any kind of TB while riding the bus. But if you live in a shelter or a prison, or if you share a room with a hospital patient who has TB, you may. If that person has multi-drug-resistant TB, and you become infected, the usual antibiotics will not cure you.

People have been suffering from tuberculosis for thousands of years. A single untreatable person who is left at large can cause many new cases and deaths over a period of time. Should we turn to sanatoriums again to isolate these people? Some experts think so. Everyone agrees that some kind of isolation or quarantine is necessary for those who cannot be persuaded to take medication regularly.

The 1994 report of a steep drop in new TB cases in New York City, and the decline nationwide, shows that the disease can be controlled by increased funding and the work of health departments across the United States. But there is still an increase in some cities and in many parts of the world.

In July 1994, it was reported that 23 percent of the students in La Quinta High School, Westminster, California, tested positive for TB. Twelve of them had active cases of multi-drug-resistant tuberculosis. Seventy other students, who were exposed to drug-resistant strains, received preventive medicines. One student, who had an active case, lost part of her lung. California officials, who are concerned about the spread of tuberculosis, have begun a $17 million plan for tuberculosis control and elimination. All students entering kindergarten, sixth, and ninth grades will be tested, and there will increased monitoring in high risk areas, like prisons and homeless shelters, too.

If you know about tuberculosis, you can help others to understand that now is the time to make certain that people with active tuberculosis be identified, that they get medical help, and that they be prevented from spreading the disease.

Glossary

active tuberculosis: a form of the disease in which there are symptoms; contagious until medication begins to take effect

AIDS (acquired immunodeficiency syndrome): a disease that destroys a person's natural defenses against other diseases

bacteria: microscopic organisms that exist in a wide variety of forms. Some kinds of bacteria cause diseases, such as tuberculosis, syphilis, and typhoid fever.

BCG (Bacillus Calmette-Guérin): a vaccine used to prevent TB. It is most common in foreign countries. Effectiveness varies.

Black Death: bubonic plague, a bacterial illness that was usually fatal before antibiotics were developed. There were many severe plague epidemics.

consumption: an old-fashioned name for tuberculosis

contact investigation: interviews, counseling, education, examination, and investigation directed at persons who have been in close contact with patients who have infectious TB

detention: temporary confinement of a person who has or who is suspected of having multi-drug-resistant TB

directly observed therapy (DOT): treatment in which health care providers or other assigned persons observe patients taking anti-TB medications

drug resistance: ability of a microbe to survive and multiply even in the presence of a drug that would ordinarily disable or kill it

exposure: the sharing of air with a person who has TB

HIV (human immunodeficiency virus): the cause of AIDS. The virus may not cause symptoms for ten or more years, but a person who is infected can spread the virus.

infectious TB: TB that can be transmitted to others, as determined by a chest X ray, test of sputum, or other tests

isoniazid: a drug commonly used in the treatment of TB

lupus: a form of tuberculosis that affects the skin

Mantoux test: a test for TB that uses purified tuberculin extract injected under the skin. Swelling shows the presence of TB, but a person may not have other symptoms.

microbe: See *microorganism*

microorganism: a form of life too small to be seen by the naked eye

miliary TB: a generalized infection in which TB germs are spread through the bloodstream

multi-drug-resistant TB: tuberculosis that is not curable by the usual antibiotics

Mycobacterium tuberculosis complex: the complex of microbe species that causes tuberculosis. Includes avian, bovine, and other forms

pneumothorax: an operation to collapse a lung by pumping air into the chest

PPD (purified protein derivative): a substance used in a skin test for TB

Pott's disease: tuberculosis of the vertebrae of the spine

pulmonary TB: tuberculosis of the lungs, the most common form

pyrazinamide: a drug commonly used in the treatment of TB

quarantine: a limit on the movement of persons exposed to,

or infected with, TB. Intended to prevent the exposure of other persons

rifampin: a drug commonly used in the treatment of TB

scrofula: TB of the lymph nodes

tine test: a test for TB in which purified tuberculin is inserted into the skin by a multipronged device

tuberculin: a liquid extracted from the tubercle bacillus

tuberculin skin test: a method of demonstrating infection with TB

tubercle bacillus: term used to refer to the germ that causes TB

tuberculosis: an infectious disease caused by bacteria known as *Mycobacterium*; it may affect almost any organ of the body

tuberculosis meningitis: TB of the brain and spinal cord

virus: the smallest infectious particle. It depends on cells in living hosts

White Plague: a name given to tuberculosis, especially of the lung

For More Information

Contact your local health association and your local branch of the American Lung Association. Most phone books list them on the page that covers community services associations, and also under "Health Agencies" in the yellow pages.

You may obtain further information from the following:

American Lung Association
1740 Broadway
New York, NY 10019
(212) 315-8700

Centers for Disease Control
Division of Tuberculosis
  Elimination
1600 Clifton Road NE
Atlanta, GA 30333
(404) 639-33111

National Jewish Center for Immunology and Respiratory Medicine
1400 Jackson Street
Denver, CO 80206
(800) 222-LUNG

Index